Ares and the
Spear of Fear

DON'T MISS THE OTHER ADVENTURES
IN THE HEROES IN TRAINING SERIES!

Zeus and the Thunderbolt of Doom

Poseidon and the Sea of Fury

Hades and the Helm of Darkness

Hyperion and the Great Balls of Fire

Typhon and the Winds of Destruction

Apollo and the Battle of the Birds

COMING SOON:

Cronus and the Threads of Dread

HEROES IN TRAINING

Ares and the Spear of Fear

Joan Holub and
Suzanne Williams

Aladdin

NEW YORK   LONDON
TORONTO   SYDNEY   NEW DELHI

ALADDIN

An imprint of Simon & Schuster Children's Publishing Division
1230 Avenue of the Americas, New York, NY 10020
First Aladdin hardcover edition August 2014
Text copyright © 2014 by Joan Holub and Suzanne Williams
Illustrations copyright © 2014 by Craig Phillips
Also available in an Aladdin paperback edition.

For information about special discounts for bulk purchases,
please contact Simon & Schuster Special Sales
at 1-866-506-1949 or business@simonandschuster.com.
The Simon & Schuster Speakers Bureau can bring authors to your live event.
For more information or to book an event,
contact the Simon & Schuster Speakers Bureau at 1-866-248-3049
or visit our website at www.simonspeakers.com.
Jacket designed by Karin Paprocki
Interior designed by Mike Rosamilia
The text of this book was set in Adobe Garamond Pro.
Manufactured in the United States of America 0714 FFG
2 4 6 8 10 9 7 5 3 1
This book has been cataloged with the Library of Congress.
ISBN 978-1-4424-8849-6 (hc)
ISBN 978-1-4424-8848-9 (pbk)
ISBN 978-1-4424-8850-2 (eBook)

For readers of Heroes in Training, Goddess Girls, and Grimmtastic Girls
—J. H. and S. W.

⚡ Contents ⚡

Greetings,
Mortal Readers,

I am Pythia, the Oracle of Delphi, in Greece. I have the power to see the future. Hear my prophecy:

Ahead I see donkeys lurking. Wait—make that *danger* lurking. (The future can be blurry, especially when my eyeglasses are foggy.)

Anyhoo, beware! Titan giants seek to rule all of Earth's domains—oceans, mountains, forests, and the depths of the Underwear. Oops—make that *Underworld*. Led by King Cronus, they are out to destroy us all!

Yet I foresee hope. A band of rightful rulers called Olympians will arise. Though their size and youth are no match for the Titans, they will be giant in heart, mind, and spirit. They await their leader—a very special boy. One who is destined to become king of the gods and ruler of the heavens.

If he is brave enough.

And if he and his friends work together as one. And if they can learn to use their new amazing flowers—um, amazing *powers*—in time to save the world!

CHAPTER ONE

On the Run

Scrubby plants brushed against Zeus's legs as he raced across the top of the mountain. Behind him, he could hear the grunts of the half-giant Cronies as they chased him and the other Olympians across the sandy ground.

Zeus risked a quick look behind him. The size and bulk of the Cronies, plus the armored chest plates they wore, were slowing the half-giants down. Hera and Poseidon were right behind

1

Zeus, with Apollo behind them and Ares bringing up the rear.

There should have been three more Olympians with them, but the Crony army had captured Hestia, Demeter, and Hades. Zeus tried not to think about that now. He couldn't save anybody if the Cronies captured him, too.

"We should stand and fight!" Ares yelled.

"You've never fought Cronies before!" Zeus replied, looking back at Ares. He was the newest member of the Olympians. Ares had lived with a family of giant Titans his whole life up till now. "We may not be stronger than they are, but we're always faster. We just— *Oof!*"

Zeus tripped over a rock and fell facedown onto the ground. Before he could get back to his feet, he felt a hand grip each of his arms.

Hera and Poseidon had grabbed him. They pulled him up. These two Olympians—along with Hades, Hestia, and Demeter—were Zeus's brothers and sisters. (Although, they had only just found this out.) Even though Apollo wasn't their brother, he had joined the group like he was one of them too. His singing rhymes were both funny and kind of annoying!

"Nice move, Bolt Breath!" Hera teased.

"I didn't see it!" Zeus protested.

"Um, guys—still running!" Poseidon called back, jogging ahead of them.

Apollo caught up to them. *"I see some trees up on the right. If we hide there we'll be out of sight,"* sang the blond-haired boy.

"How can you rhyme at a time like this?" Hera asked, rolling her blue eyes.

"Hiding in the trees is a good idea. Let's go!" Zeus cried.

They veered toward the right and headed into the stand of trees. Zeus came to a stop, panting.

"We need a plan," he said. "There are four half-giant Cronies chasing us, but there's a whole army of them in the canyon below. They won't stop until they find us."

"We need Pythia," Poseidon said, frowning. The Oracle of Delphi always showed up to tell them what to do next. But after they'd found Ares, she hadn't appeared.

"That's why we've got to lose these half-giants and get to Delphi," Zeus told him.

Ares's red eyes flashed. "Forget losing them. Let's attack them!"

"These guys don't go down easily," Zeus said. "And even if we defeat the first four, there's a whole army behind them."

"Shhh!" Hera warned, quickly darting behind a tree. "I think they're close-by."

Apollo, Poseidon, and Zeus all scrambled to hide behind trees too. But not Ares. He raised his spear and charged through the trees, screaming so loudly that the sound echoed through the hills.

"I am Ares the Olympian! Feel my anger!" he yelled. "We shall not be defeated!"

"Oh no," Hera whispered. "Is he serious?"

He was. Zeus thought Ares looked pretty ferocious as he sped through the trees with his sharp spear, spiky brown hair, and weird, fiery eyes. But Zeus knew that Ares didn't stand a chance against the Cronies on his own. He darted out from behind the tree.

"Zeus, don't!" Hera hissed.

"He's one of us," Zeus reminded her. "We've got to help him."

Hera sighed. *"Fine."*

Zeus, Hera, Poseidon, and Apollo raced after Ares. They found him standing just outside the trees, frozen in fear as he stared at the approaching Cronies. Zeus couldn't blame him. Each Crony was about eight feet tall and massively muscled. They brandished clubs, spears, and sharp arrows.

Zeus grabbed him. "Come on, Ares. Let's stick to the plan."

"Wh-what plan?" Ares asked, his bottom lip trembling.

"Run!" Zeus yelled.

The chase began again. The Olympians raced off along the edge of the mountain ridge. Somewhere down below, Zeus knew, was the rest of King Cronus's army.

"You can't escape us, Olympians!" one of the Cronies bellowed. Zeus saw Ares turn pale as he ran by his side.

Ares can talk a good talk, Zeus thought. *But can he back it up?*

The Olympians quickly gained another lead

on the Cronies. But then Poseidon came to a quick halt up ahead of Zeus.

"Hold on, guys!" Poseidon yelled.

Zeus suddenly realized why Poseidon had stopped. The Cronies had chased them to a dead end—a narrow ledge overlooking the canyon. Zeus ran to the edge and looked over. The canyon wall was too steep to climb down, and too high to jump from. Deep, rocky craters and sharp boulders dotted the landscape below.

Hera, Apollo, and Ares arrived next, panting.

"We're done for!" Ares wailed, looking down.

"Yup, sure seems that way," Hera agreed.

The five of them turned to face the Cronies. One of them had a big scar across his face.

"We've got you now!" he growled.

Poseidon leaned toward his friends. "Trust me, guys," he whispered. He held up his trident,

the magical object that belonged to him as the god of the sea.

"Poseidon, what are you doing?" Zeus asked.

"Jumping," Poseidon replied.

With that, he launched himself over the edge of the cliff.

CHAPTER TWO

Old Enemies Return

eus watched in horror as Poseidon disappeared over the edge.

"What a scaredy-cat!" one of the Cronies sneered as those half-giants pushed toward the Olympians.

Hera grabbed Zeus's hand. "He said to trust him."

Zeus nodded. "Right."

"No way!" Ares cried, but Hera grabbed his hand too.

"Too bad," she said. "You're coming with us!"

Apollo began to sing. *"If we're going to jump, let's do it now, before those Cronies start to—* Whoaaaaaa!"

Hera and Zeus jumped off the top of the cliff, taking Ares and Apollo with them. Everything happened in a matter of seconds, but to the Olympians it felt like slow motion.

As they were falling, Zeus knew he shouldn't do it, but he looked down—and saw Poseidon splashing into a deep pool of water.

He must have made it with his trident! Zeus realized.

Then Zeus felt Hera yank on his belt. He looked down to see her pulling out Bolt, his magical lightning bolt.

"No!" Zeus yelled, watching as Hera tossed Bolt away.

Splash! Splash! Splash! Splash! Zeus, Hera, Apollo, and Ares landed safely in the deep pool of water.

"Play dead!" Poseidon urged the others. He floated on his stomach with his face in the water.

Zeus took a deep breath and did the same. He held his breath until he felt like he would burst. Then he lifted his head, gasping for air.

"It's okay," he heard Hera say. "They're gone."

Ares was already climbing out of the pool. "Are you crazy?" he yelled, pointing his spear at Poseidon.

"Would you rather have been captured by the Cronies?" Poseidon shot back.

At the same time, Zeus was yelling at Hera.

"What did you do with Bolt?" he asked.

"Bolt is *electric*. And this is water," Hera pointed out. "Do I have to spell it out for you? We would have been fried."

"Oh," Zeus said a little sheepishly.

"Besides, you can call it back to you whenever you want," she reminded him.

Zeus nodded and held out his hand. "Bolt! Return!"

The small lightning bolt zipped through the air and then settled right into Zeus's hand. He slipped it back into his belt.

"That army is not far away. We should escape without delay," Apollo rhyme-reminded them.

Zeus knew Apollo was right. He scanned the horizon.

"I think there might be some caves over there," he said, pointing to a rocky cliff side in the distance. "Let's head that way."

Wet and exhausted, they headed down the canyon. A few minutes later Zeus spotted a cave halfway up the side of the cliff, and they scrambled up to it.

"We should be safe here for a little while," he said.

"Can you use that lightning thing of yours to make a fire?" Ares asked with a shiver. "I wouldn't mind drying off."

"Too dangerous," Hera replied. "The Cronies could spot it."

Ares sighed and folded his arms across his chest. "So, what do we do now?"

"We figure out the best way to lose the Cronies, and then we get to Delphi and find Pythia," Zeus told him.

Hera held up a piece of oval stone she wore around her neck on a cord. "Chip will get us there," she said confidently.

"So, what does that thing do?" Ares asked.

"Chip always know which way we're supposed to go," she answered. "And it can talk when it wants to, in its own language."

Ares nodded. "So how did you find it?"

Hera's face colored, and Zeus answered for her.

"I found it, actually, at the temple of Delphi," he said. "Where I found Bolt. Hera's been taking care of it for me, along with Hades's helm."

"Hera and I don't have our own magical objects yet," Apollo informed Ares. He motioned to the stringed instrument that he carried over his shoulder. "My lyre makes beautiful music, but it's not magical."

"Well, I don't need any magic," Ares said, holding up his metal-tipped wood spear. "I'll use this to fight off any Crony that comes close!"

"Yeah, as long as you're not frozen in place," Poseidon muttered.

Ares spun around, his red eyes flashing. "What did you say?"

"Shhhh!" Hera warned suddenly. "Do you hear that?"

A rumbling sound was rising from the canyon below. The Olympians peeked out of the cave and saw that the whole Crony army had gathered there. Two of the Cronies were chasing a giant urn, which was rolling away.

"Nice job dropping it, Ephialtes!" said one of the Cronies, a huge, oafish-looking half-giant with a bald head.

"You're the one who dropped it, Otus!" shot back Ephialtes, a Crony with a big belly.

"What's so important about that urn?" Poseidon wondered out loud.

"*That urn is big enough to hide—three lost Olympian friends inside*," sang Apollo.

Hera's eyes got wide. "They just might be in there!" she cried. "We have to rescue them!"

"But we don't know for sure," Zeus pointed out. "And besides, the whole army is guarding that urn. We can't fight them. That's why we've

got to find Pythia. She'll tell us what to do."

The Olympians heard loud voices drift up to the cave, and Zeus saw three Cronies down below. He'd know them anywhere; they were the ones who had captured him right before he found Bolt and discovered the other Olympians. He'd nicknamed the three Cronies: Double Chin (for his double chin), Blackbeard (for his black beard), and Lion Tattoo (for the tattoo of a lion on his shoulder).

"Those two bumbling blockheads need to take better care of that urn," growled Lion Tattoo, the leader. "King Cronus's belly is empty, and a dozen Olympians would fill it up good."

"A dozen!" Zeus exclaimed in a whisper. He looked at Hera. "Could there really be that many of us?"

Hera shrugged. "I guess. Pythia never told us."

Ares was pale. "What did he mean, '*King*

Cronus's belly is empty'?" Does the king actually *eat* Olympians?"

"He swallowed me, Hera, and Hades when we were little," Poseidon explained. "Zeus made him barf us up."

Hera shuddered. "It was like a dark, smelly cave in his belly. Perfect for Hades, but I really don't want to go back there."

"No kidding," said Ares. "That's why we've got to battle these guys and defeat this army!"

"Yeah, you suggested that before," Poseidon reminded him. "Didn't work out so well, did it?"

Ares's eyes flashed again. "Those are fighting words!" he yelled.

"Ares, sshh!" Hera hissed, but it was too late.

Lion Tattoo's head snapped around. He grinned, pointing up to their cave.

"Olympians!" he yelled.

"They've spotted us!" Zeus cried. "Run!"

CHAPTER THREE

Snakes Alive!

Zeus knew they had one advantage: they had already scaled up the side of the cliff to get to the cave. The slow-moving Cronies would have a hard time catching up to them.

"To the top of the cliff!" Zeus yelled, and the others followed him, scrambling the rest of the way up the cliff side. Zeus could see a forest of pine trees ahead, and he led the group toward the canopy—and protection—of the trees. The angry cries of the Cronies rose up behind them as those half-giants struggled to scale the cliff.

Other travelers had already worn a path through the forest, and the Olympians raced down it, not daring to look behind them. After what seemed like forever, they came to a fork in the path and stopped, all trying to catch their breath.

"Which way?" Zeus wondered out loud.

Poseidon sniffed the air. "I smell salt water. If we go right, we should reach the channel. Crossing the channel is the fastest way to Delphi."

"Then that's where we'll go," Zeus said.

"It seems to me there is a way. To lead the Crony army astray," rhymed Apollo.

Poseidon sighed. "Can you just please say what you mean?"

"I mean, we could leave some sort of object by

the left path, to trick the Cronies into thinking we went down it so they will follow the wrong path," Apollo said cheerfully.

Hera nodded. "Good idea. Maybe a scrap of tunic? Or some breadcrumbs? Or— HEY!"

Hera turned to see Zeus holding a lock of her long, golden hair. He had cut a piece off with Bolt!

"Perfect!" Zeus said, grinning. He placed the lock of hair on a tree branch by the entrance to the left-hand path.

Hera glared at him. "Do that again, and I'll shave you bald, Thunderboy!"

Suddenly they heard the sound of the Cronies charging down the path behind them.

"Let's go!" Zeus yelled.

The Olympians headed down the right path and didn't stop until they emerged from the forest. A sloping hill in front of them led down to a sandy seashore. Sun glittered on the surface of the water.

"Hear that?" Hera asked. Aside from the breathing of the Olympians, the lapping of the waves against the shore, and the hoot of an owl in the distance, the sloping hill was quiet.

"We lost them!" Poseidon cheered. He gave Zeus a high five. "Nice work, Bro!"

"Hey, it was *my* hair," Hera reminded him.

Poseidon high-fived her, too. "I'm just glad to be away from those Cronies."

"They'll figure it out soon enough," Zeus said. "Anyway, how are we supposed to cross this sea channel? Swim?"

"Fishermen usually leave their boats on the shore," Ares said, heading down the hill. "Come on! We can borrow one."

"Stealing isn't nice, you know. Is there another way to go?" sang Apollo.

"Apollo, it's a matter of life and death!" Hera insisted. "I'm sure the fisherman would understand if he knew."

Apollo frowned. "I suppose," he said reluctantly.

They followed Ares down to the moonlit shore.

"Yes! Just like I thought!" Ares exclaimed. A row of rickety boats were neatly lined up on the beach. Ares ran over to one and started pushing it into the water.

"Climb in!" he urged.

They climbed in, and Poseidon took the oars first, smiling.

"Water, at last," he said. "You guys should get some sleep. I'll wake you when I get tired."

"Do we have anything to eat?" Ares asked. "I'm so hungry, I could eat a Crony's smelly sandal."

"We still have some of the food those grateful farmers gave us a few days ago after we helped them regrow their crops, but we should probably save it for the morning," Hera said.

Poseidon grinned. "Don't worry. I'll make sure there's a great breakfast waiting for us when we wake up. Trust me."

Soon the rest of the Olympians were dozing, and after Poseidon had rowed for a while, the others took turns rowing through the night. The sun was rising as the boat reached the opposite shore.

When they woke up, they saw Poseidon proudly holding up a string of fish.

"I caught them myself," he bragged. "It's a god-of-the-sea thing. These fish practically jumped into the boat. Bro, a little fire, maybe?"

"No problem," Zeus said. He gathered some dried seaweed and made a fire on the shore using a spark from his thunder-dagger, Bolt.

Before long they were eating the delicious fish.

"Now, that's what I call breakfast!" Poseidon said, licking his lips.

Hera leaned back and gazed at the blue water of the channel, sparkling in the morning sun. "I wish we didn't always have to run," she said with a sigh.

"I know, but Hades, Hestia, and Demeter need us," Zeus said impatiently. "Come on. We've got to go. It's a day's walk to Delphi."

They all knew Zeus was right. So they climbed to their feet and began the long walk to the temple at Delphi to search for the oracle, Pythia. They stopped only to eat some of the farmers' fruit and cheese from their packs when the sun was high in the blue sky.

A few hours later Zeus saw the white columns of the Delphi temple rising on a hill in the distance. He stopped.

"There it is," he said, and memories came

flooding back to him. Getting Bolt and Chip, meeting the other Olympians, fighting Titans and Cronies—this was where his adventure had started.

"Should we just walk up to it?" Hera asked. "What if the Cronies beat us to it and are guarding it?"

Zeus nodded to the invisibility helmet Hera was carrying. "Maybe you can make like Hades and find out."

"What? Oh, sure," Hera said, realizing what her brother meant. She slipped on Hades' helmet and immediately became invisible.

"Be right back," she said.

The boys anxiously waited for her.

"I hope Pythia is okay," Apollo said worriedly. "It's not like her to do a disappearing act like this."

"I know," Zeus agreed.

"Well, if this Pythia tells us to battle, then I

am ready!" Ares said, waving his spear around.

Poseidon opened his mouth to say something insulting, but Zeus stopped him with a look. The Cronies were already fighting them. The Olympians didn't need to fight one another, too.

Suddenly Hera appeared in front of them again.

"Well, I did a circle around the temple," she said. "No sign of Cronies. Or Pythia, either."

"She must be inside," Zeus said. "She's got to be. Let's go."

They walked up the hill toward the temple. *It really is magnificent*, Zeus thought. Shaped like a cylinder, it stood on a platform ringed with tall, white marble columns. Its inner chamber was surrounded by marble walls, and the whole structure was topped with a red stone roof.

The Olympians cautiously started up the marble steps.

"Pythia?" Zeus called out. He tried to see inside the inner chamber, but all he could make out was darkness.

Sssssssssssss.

"What's that?" Ares asked, jumping back.

Sssssssssss.

"Snakes alive!" yelled Poseidon.

An enormous python snake slithered out from the inner chamber toward them. The Olympians raced back down the stairs, hearts pounding.

The snake's body was as thick as one of the marble columns. Its shimmering brown scales were highlighted by a pattern of gold markings. Two glossy black eyes as big as dinner plates stared menacingly at the Olympians, and a red tongue darted from its mouth.

"Who isss it?" the python asked as its impossibly long body slithered around the columns. "Who dares disssturb the greatessst python who

has ever lived? The ssslitheriest ssserpent who has ever hisssed?"

"That is one stuck-up snake!" Poseidon remarked.

Suddenly a black-haired woman wearing glasses appeared in the entrance to the chamber.

"Pythia!" Zeus yelled.

"Don't worry about me, Juice—I mean, Zeus!" she called out. "The python has me trapped here, but I'm fine. However, I need to send you on a new, urgent quest. Right now. Pronto!"

"You are in great danger, we all fear. You cannot let us leave you here!" Apollo sang.

"I don't plan to leave her here," Zeus said firmly. "We're going to rescue her."

"On it!" Ares said, brandishing his spear. "It's battle time!"

Then he charged up the stairs, right at the snake!

CHAPTER FOUR

A Fierce Foe

Before Ares could get near the python, it lashed out and wrapped around his body. Then the python gleefully slid around the columns, dragging Ares along with it.

Crack! Ares's spear hit one of the columns and snapped in two. He was left with a short, broken stick in his hand.

"You think you can harm me with a ssspear?" the snake hissed. "What a sssilly boy you are!"

"We have to help him!" Hera cried.

The python released its grip on Ares and tossed him into the air. Then it caught him again before he could hit the ground.

"Whooaaaaaa!" Ares wailed.

"Bolt, large!" Zeus commanded, and in an instant the lightning bolt grew as tall as him. He turned to Poseidon, who raised his trident high.

"Get ready for an awesome combo, snake!" Poseidon yelled as he moved to touch the trident to Bolt. They had discovered by accident that when the magical objects touched each other, they gave off a big burst of power.

But before the objects could meet . . . *Whack!* The serpent lashed out again, knocking Poseidon and Zeus off their feet. The boys lost their grips on their weapons as they went flying backward—snapping off part of Ares's half-spear.

The snake tossed Ares into the air again. When it wrapped around him once more, Ares started poking the snake with his broken stick.

"Take that! And that!" he yelled. But the python just giggled.

"That tickles-s-s!" the snake hissed.

Hera's blue eyes lit up, and she picked up a random feather she'd spotted on the steps. The green feather had blue and orange markings on the end that looked like an eye.

"A peacock feather," she murmered to herself. "Perfect for tickling!"

She raced up the steps and started tickling the python's belly.

"Ha-ha-ha-ha!" the snake laughed. "Ssstop it!"

Several yards away Zeus slowly sat up in the grass. The snake had knocked the wind out of him. He looked down at his empty right hand.

"Bolt! Return!" he yelled, and the magical lightning bolt zipped back into his palm.

That's when he heard the voices behind him.

"I can't believe they won't let us carry the urn no more."

"I know! Just 'cause we dropped it a bunch of times. No fair."

Zeus turned to see the two Cronies Otus and Ephialtes cresting the hill behind him. Their loud, deep voices carried down the hill.

"And then they sent us out here on a wild duck chase," said Otus. "Looking for lost Olympians."

"I think it's called a wild goose chase," Ephialtes said.

"Whatever," said Otus. "I don't see no geese here, though. No Olympians, either. Just some boy holding a lightning bolt."

Ephialtes squinted down the hill. "Hey, ain't he an Olympian?" he asked, pointing at Zeus.

Zeus ran toward the temple as fast as he could. He had to warn the others!

"The Cronies have found us!" he yelled as he raced up the steps.

Meanwhile, under the tickle-feather, the python couldn't control itself any longer. "Ha-ha-ha. Hee-hee-hee. Nooo!" He giggled, letting go of his grip on Ares. The red-eyed boy landed with a thud on the stairs. Apollo helped him get to his feet.

Ares turned to Hera, angry. "Why did you butt in? I was just about to get him where I wanted him!"

"You're welcome," Hera said in a huff, rolling her eyes and tucking the peacock feather in her belt.

"Did anybody hear me? We've got Cronies on our tail!" Zeus yelled.

"Run!" Pythia called out from inside the

chamber. "Your next quest is to find the Spear of Fear. A group of warmongering girls called Amazons possesses it, but it truly belongs to Ares, god of war."

"Woo-hoo!" Ares cheered, pumping his fist in the air.

"But what about Hades, Hestia, and Demeter?" Zeus asked. "They've been captured!"

"You must first find the spear. That is my strongest vision. Do that, and all will fall into place," she replied. "As for me, I'll be fine against this blowhard python. It's really just full of hot air!"

Annoyed, the python slid back inside the chamber and started chasing Pythia around. At that moment, Otus and Ephialtes appeared at the bottom of the temple stairs.

"Olympians! Four of them!" Otus yelled.

Four? Zeus thought. There was him, Apollo,

Ares, Hera, and Poseidon . . . Poseidon? He didn't see his sea-god brother anywhere.

"Poseidon!" Zeus yelled.

"I haven't seen him since the snake tossed him," Hera said.

"Go!" Pythia ordered from inside the temple. "Now is not the time to help me or your missing friends!"

Zeus hated to leave without Poseidon, but he knew he had no choice. He quickly aimed Bolt at the two approaching Cronies and zapped them both.

"Ow! Ow!" they complained, jumping up and down.

"Let's go!" Zeus called.

The four Olympians ran around the temple and headed downstairs when they reached the other side. The python stuck its head out of the temple as they passed. The sharp end of the broken spear was sticking out of its mouth.

"Thanksss for the toothpick!" it said with a laugh.

"I'll be back for you, or my name isn't Ares, god of war!" Ares shouted, shaking his fist at the snake.

But the snake just grinned.

"Ssso long, losersss!"

CHAPTER FIVE

The Amazons

I t didn't take the Olympians long to lose Otus and Ephialtes. But even though he, Hera, Apollo, and Ares were safe, Zeus felt awful.

"We shouldn't have left Poseidon behind," he kept repeating as they made their way along a dirt road.

"Poseidon is safe, I must believe. Or Pythia would not have let us leave," Apollo rhymed.

"Yeah," agreed Ares. "Besides, he was always

bragging about how brave he was. He can take care of himself."

"No Olympian left behind," Zeus muttered, kicking a stone with his sandal.

Hera put a hand on his shoulder. "I miss him too. But Pythia hasn't steered us wrong yet."

Zeus sighed. "I know." He pointed at the peacock feather tucked into Hera's belt. "Hey, nice work with that thing, tickling the snake."

Hera smiled. "Thanks. I got lucky finding the feather. I'm going to hang on to it. Peacock feathers can mean good or bad luck, depending on who's holding them. This one was definitely good luck for us," she said. "Besides, it's really beautiful, isn't it?"

"Yeah, it is," Zeus agreed.

Then Hera's smile faded. "It feels weird with only four of us. How will we ever find all the Olympians if we keep losing them along the way?"

"I guess we just have to stick to Pythia's plan and trust it'll work," Zeus replied. "Can you use Chip to help us find the land of the Amazons?"

"They live in the Scythian Mountains," Apollo informed them. "It'll take us weeks to get there."

Hera groaned. "Of course. Nothing is ever easy with Pythia."

Ares turned to face them. "Well, I'm going, even if I have to go alone! That spear is mine! With it I'll inspire fear in my enemies! I'll be the greatest warrior ever!" he crowed.

"Nobody's going off alone again," Zeus said firmly. "We'll stick together all the way to the Scythian Mountains, no matter how long it takes."

Hera held Chip in the palm of her hand. A green arrow appeared on the stone, pointing north.

"Onward!" Hera cried out.

They walked all afternoon, and Apollo made up songs as they traveled.

"The four Olympians walked and walked.
They walked and walked some more.
They walked and walked and walked and walked,
Those brave Olympians four."

"I don't know, Apollo," Hera said, shaking her head. "That was a little . . . repetitive."

"Well, we aren't doing much besides walking," Apollo said with a shrug. "What else am I supposed to sing about?"

"Maybe that shiny aegis?" Ares teased. "I have never seen a shield so gold and shiny. And the tassels! What kind of weird armor is that?"

Apollo looked down at the aegis he wore. "I think it's kind of impressive."

"If you're going to a costume party," Ares said, snorting. "Ha!"

They kept going until just before sundown, when they made camp under a rocky ledge. Their food was running out, but they managed a meal of some leftover carrots and cheese crumbles that had fallen to the bottom of Hera's pack.

"I wouldn't mind some of Poseidon's fish right now," Ares said.

"I don't care about the fish," Zeus said. "I just miss Poseidon."

Apollo slipped off the aegis. "This thing sure is heavy," he said. "I'm not sure if I want to keep wearing it."

Ares quickly grabbed it. "I'll take it!"

Apollo frowned. "I thought you didn't like it! You think it's silly."

"I never said that," Ares said quickly. "Anyway, it's mine now."

He was probably teasing Apollo earlier just so he could get the shield for himself, Zeus decided. *After all, the god of war would probably need one.*

"We still don't know whose magical object it is," Zeus reminded Ares. "It could be for one of our friends, or an Olympian we haven't met yet. So you'll have to give it up when the time comes."

"No problem," Ares said, slipping the shield over his chest.

"Are you actually going to sleep in that?" Hera asked.

"I'm a warrior," Ares replied. "That's what we do."

Hera shook her head. "Okay, whatever."

The four Olympians all fell asleep very quickly, tired from a long day. As the group's leader, Zeus always slept lightly. Because they never knew when Cronies might try to attack. Right at sunrise Zeus thought he heard footsteps, and bolted awake.

"Don't move, Cronies!" a loud voice commanded.

Zeus stood up. "Cronies? Where?"

Eight girls now surrounded their camp. Each girl's hair was braided down her back, and each one held a long, metal-tipped spear. And each spear was pointed at the four Olympians.

"Don't move!" warned one of the girls, a tall one with dark eyes.

Zeus put his hands above his head. "I won't! But where are the Cronies?"

Hera, Apollo, and Ares were awake by now.

"Um, I think they think *we're* the Cronies," Hera told him.

"Ha! I thought King Cronus was forming great armies," said the dark-eyed girl. "His soldiers are everywhere, and said to be fierce. But none of you Cronies have anything to fight with except that bolt."

"Well, we are still fierce," Hera protested. "But we aren't Cronies. We're all fighting King Cronus. We're Olympians."

"All you have is a helmet and a feather," said another girl. "She can't be a Crony."

The other girls looked to the dark-eyed girl, who seemed to be their leader. She nodded, and they lowered their spears.

"Welcome," she said. "I am Eurybe. We are Amazons."

Hera jumped up. "No way! We were looking for you," she said. "It's really good luck that we found you."

"Maybe your peacock feather is good luck after all," Zeus said.

"Of course it is," Hera snapped. "I already told you that."

Eurybe looked at Hera. "What are you doing with all these stinky boys anyway?"

"I told you, we're Olympians," Hera said. "It's our destiny to defeat King Cronus. And you can help us. Have you ever heard of the Spear of Fear?"

The Amazon warriors started laughing. "Yeah," said one of the Amazons.

"I'm the god of war, and it's my rightful weapon," Ares said. "What's so funny?"

"Your face," Eurybe said teasingly, and then she turned to Hera. "Seriously, blond girl, you should come fight King Cronus with us. There are no boys in the Amazon tribe. We don't need them. What do you say?"

Hera looked delighted and proud to be asked. For a second Zeus worried that she might accept their invitation.

"That sounds pretty cool," said Hera. "But I need to stay with my friends. Olympians stick together."

Eurybe shook her head. "Stick together with boys? Yuck! But it's your choice."

She nodded to one of the Amazons. The girl pulled a spear from a strap on her back and hurled it toward Ares. It landed in the ground and fell right between his feet.

"Here's your spear," Eurybe said, and the girls laughed again.

Ares pulled the spear from the ground. It didn't look very amazing. The shaft was made of rusty iron, with pieces flaking off here and there. The point was flat and dull.

"Are you sure this is it?" Ares asked.

"Maybe it just looks harmless so it fools your enemies," Zeus suggested.

That made the Amazons laugh even harder.

"Have fun with that spear!" Eurybe called out, and then she and the other Amazons swiftly ran off.

"I still don't understand what's so funny!" Ares fumed.

"*It is good luck that we found the spear, but something is amiss, I fear,*" Apollo sang.

"They're just a bunch of silly girls," Ares said. He held the spear over his head. "It's all good. Because the god of war now has the Spear of Fear!"

CHAPTER SIX

Scaredy-Spear

T hree cheers for the spear!" Zeus yelled. "Now we don't have to walk all the way to the Scythian Mountains. We can go rescue Pythia and the rest of the Olympians!"

"Hooray!" cheered Hera, Ares, and Apollo.

"Let's get moving!" Ares said, jabbing his spear into the air. "I can't wait to show that rotten snake what the god of war is really made of!"

They quickly got back to the road.

"I can't believe how easy this was," Zeus said, feeling more cheerful with each step. "Remember what we went through the get Demeter's seeds? We had to climb a beanstalk, battle a giant, and run from giant bees. But this time we got the magical object handed right to us!"

"Thanks to my peacock feather," Hera said proudly, giving it a pat. "I know it's bringing us good luck."

Zeus sighed. She kept bringing up that peacock feather every time something good happened. He was getting a little sick of hearing about it. But he knew it would probably just make her mad again if he said anything.

She might be my sister, but most of the time I just don't get her, he thought.

Ares kept waving the spear around.

"Take that! And that!" he yelled at invisible enemies.

Apollo strummed his lyre, whispering new song lyrics to himself as they walked.

Suddenly Chip, the oval stone that hung on a cord around Hera's neck, cried out, "Anger-dip! Ronies-Cip ear-nip!"

Chip spoke his own language: Chip Latin. By now all of the Olympians understood it.

"Cronies are near!" Zeus cried. "We need to hide."

Luckily, they were passing a hay field, and they all found a hiding spot in the tall grass. Zeus dared to peek through it, and saw Otus and Ephialtes plodding up the road toward them.

"We've been looking and looking, but no Olympians," complained Otus.

"I know. My feet hurt!" moaned Ephialtes.

Ares pushed past Zeus. "Now's my chance to see what this spear can do!" he hissed.

"Ares, wait!" Zeus cried, but the hotheaded Olympian was already running out to the road.

"Behold the Spear of Fear!" he yelled, holding the spear above his head.

Otus and Ephialtes quickly turned toward Ares.

"It's one of them Olympians!" Otus cried.

The two half-giants stomped in Ares's direction. As they got closer, Ares took aim and threw the Spear of Fear at them.

"Show them what you can do, spear!" he yelled.

The Spear of Fear wobbled through the air for a few feet, heading toward the Cronies. But to everyone's surprise, then it boomeranged right back toward Ares and stopped to hover in the air behind his back. All of the Olympians—and even the Cronies—looked on in shock.

"The spear looks like it's *hiding*," Hera whispered to Zeus.

Ares spun around. "Spear! What gives?" He grabbed it and hurled it once again at the Cronies.

The spear just looped around again and hid

behind Ares once more, shaking now.

Ephialtes and Otus started to laugh.

"Haw! Haw! Haw!" Ephialtes bellowed. "The little Olympian has got a scaredy-spear."

Terrified and embarrassed, Ares grabbed the spear, turned, and ran back to join the other Olympians. Then he crashed through the hay and ran right past them.

Zeus raced behind him. "Good idea!"

Hera and Apollo followed them both.

Hera quickly caught up to Zeus. "We've got to lose these oafs, or they'll follow us all the way to Delphi."

"Right," Zeus agreed. He skidded to a stop. "I think I know how to slow them down."

He pulled Bolt from his belt. "Bolt, large!"

The dagger-size lightning bolt exploded to its full length. Zeus aimed it at the hay between the Olympians and the charging Cronies.

Zap! He sent sparks flying at the tall grass, and it burst into flames. The Cronies skidded to a halt.

"No fair!" Otus wailed as the flames leaped up in front of his face.

Grinning, Zeus called for Bolt to return, then ran to catch up to his friends.

"Good work," Apollo said, turning to him.

"Yeah, that'll keep those Cronies away," Hera said. "Of course, you'll burn down the whole hay field too."

Zeus felt a pang of guilt. He hadn't thought of that. "Well, Poseidon can—" he started to say, thinking of his brother's water powers. But he stopped himself. Poseidon wasn't there.

"Poseidon's not the only one who can put out a fire," Hera said. "Or do I need to remind you of that, Boltbrain?"

Zeus suddenly realized what he could do.

"You're right! Let's get to a safe place first."

"Lead us, Chip!" Hera said, looking down at the amulet.

They emerged from the hay field on another dirt path, where Chip had them make a left turn. When they were safely away from the field, Zeus called for them to stop.

"We're far enough now," he said. Zeus gazed upward. Puffy clouds were scattered across the sky, and one of them was dark gray. It just might do the trick.

"Bolt, let's jump-start that storm!" he cried, aiming Bolt at the cloud.

A jagged streak of light shot from Bolt and hit the cloud.

Boom! A loud clap of thunder rocked the sky. Big, fat raindrops began to fall from the cloud.

"Nice job," Hera admitted.

"Thanks for reminding me that I could make

storms," Zeus said. "I guess I've been a little . . . distracted lately."

He was missing Poseidon and the others so much. It had been amazing to find new brothers and sisters after growing up all alone. Losing them now just didn't seem fair.

"Spear! Come back here!" Ares yelled behind Zeus.

Zeus turned to see Ares pointing at the Spear of Fear. It had planted itself behind a bush and was shivering.

"I think it's afraid of the thunder," Apollo remarked.

"I think it's afraid of *everything*," Hera said. "That's probably why it's called the Spear of Fear. It doesn't strike fear into the hearts of its enemies. It's just full of fear! Ha! That's pretty funny."

"It is not at all funny!" Ares fumed, his eyes blazing red.

Zeus stepped between them. "I think Hera might be right, Ares. We never know how these magical objects are going to work. Let's get to Pythia and see what she says."

Ares sighed. "Fine." Instantly, the spear flew to his hand.

Chip led the way as they walked down the new road to Delphi. Apollo strummed on his lyre for a while. Then he began to sing.

"When Ares wields the Spear of Fear,
Your heart will pound and your pulse will quicken.
But when he tries to throw the spear,
You'll see that it's just a big ol' chicken!"

"Hey!" Ares protested. "Quit singing that!"

Apollo frowned. "But it took me so long to think of a word that rhymes with 'chicken.'"

"We'll see who's chicken," Ares said, waving

the spear at Apollo. The spear jumped out of his hand and hid behind Hera.

She laughed. "Oh, this is just too funny!"

"You guys are all rats!" Ares said angrily, stomping ahead of them. The spear followed him.

Zeus shook his head. "You could be a little nicer to him, you know," he said to Hera.

"Come on," Hera said. "Even you have to admit that scaredy-spear is pretty funny. Apollo, sing me more of your song."

Apollo quietly started to sing again. Zeus shook his head and sped up, hoping to catch up to Ares. He was a few feet behind when he heard Ares talking softly to the spear. Ares didn't know that Zeus could hear him.

"Don't let their laughing get to you," Ares was saying. "I'm afraid of stuff too. Lots of stuff. Like the dark. And centipedes. And Cronies. But I just *act* like I'm not afraid, and nobody knows. You gotta do that too."

Zeus nodded to himself. That made a lot of sense. Ares always acted really tough, but everyone was afraid now and then.

"You're strong," Ares was telling the spear. "You were *made* for battle. I'll train you. We can do this together."

As Zeus crept closer, he stepped on a twig, causing Ares to jump.

"Oh," Ares said, blushing. "Um, you didn't, um, hear me talking just now, did you?"

"No," Zeus lied, not wanted to embarrass his friend. "I was too busy thinking."

"Thinking about what?" Ares asked.

Zeus smiled. "Thinking about how you and your spear are going to take down that python when we get to Delphi. I know you can do it."

"Of course we can!" Ares said loudly. Then he marched down the path, more confident than Zeus had ever seen him.

CHAPTER SEVEN

Ssssneak Attack!

e'll attack at sunrise," Zeus said, drawing a map in the dirt with the stick. "The snake won't expect us back so soon, so we might have an advantage."

Stars shimmered in the sky overhead. To escape the Cronies the four Olympians had to take a longer route to Delphi. Zeus had suggested they camp for the night.

"I still think we should attack in the dark,"

Ares said, anxiously pacing back and forth at bedtime. "That snake won't see us coming!"

"Of course it will," Hera countered. "It's a python. They hunt at night."

"Exactly," Zeus agreed. "The snake would have the advantage in the dark."

"Yeah, attacking isn't all about might, you know," Hera said. "It's about strategy."

Ares sighed and sat down in front of the campfire they had built using Bolt and some nearby twigs. "Well, I'm not going to be able to sleep."

"How about a lullaby?" Apollo asked. He strummed his lyre.

"Close your eyes and go to sleep,
And tomorrow we will creep
To the temple to save the day.
And the python we will slay!

The battle will be fierce and bold.

The fight—"

"That's not helping!" Ares grumbled loudly.

"Fine," Apollo said, setting down the lyre. He yawned. "I'm tired anyway."

The four Olympians fell asleep—even Ares, but he was up before dawn and shaking the others awake just as the first rays of the sun were peeking over the horizon.

"Come on. Let's go," Ares urged them. "Let's do this!"

Zeus yawned and stretched. "Fine. By the time we get there, it'll be light."

In a few minutes they were headed to the temple, muching fruit they picked from an orchard they passed. Zeus felt excited. Once they got rid of that python, they'd be one step closer to finding the other Olympians.

"So, everyone remember the plan," Zeus said. "Apollo, Hera, and I will approach the temple from the front. Ares, you sneak around to the back. We'll distract the snake so you can attack."

"Sneak attack! All right!" Ares said, shaking his spear.

"It's a good plan, except for one thing," Hera said to Ares. "What happens when that chicken stick of yours runs and hides?"

"It won't," Ares said firmly.

"I'm not so sure about that," Hera said.

"Well, I think that the spear has been pretty smart so far," Zeus said, trying to smooth things over. "Maybe it's not afraid. Maybe it just doesn't want to make a move too soon. It's like you said before, Hera. You need strategy in battle, not just power."

"Yeah," said Ares.

"That doesn't explain why the spear is afraid of thunder," Hera pointed out.

"Everybody is afraid of something. It's normal," Zeus said, and Ares gave him a grateful look.

"And now we are here, so it's time for the spear!" Apollo rhymed.

They had reached the temple. There was no sign of the snake.

"It's probably curled up inside," Zeus said. "Okay. Here's the plan. Ares, circle around. Stay close to the trees."

"Right," Ares said, darting off.

Zeus, Hera, and Apollo marched up to the temple.

"Hey, python!" Zeus yelled. "Wake up!"

The huge head of the python slithered out from inside the temple. The snake wrapped its long body around the temple's inner chamber. He still had Ares's old wooden spear and was chomping it like it was candy.

"Well, isssn't this nice," hissed the snake. "Visitorsss. Have you come back for another round?"

"No." Zeus said firmly. "We've come back to save Pythia."

The snake laughed. "How are you going to do that? Is that yellow-haired one going to sssing to me? Is the girl going to tickle me?"

Zeus drew out Bolt. It sprang to full size. "I've got something better than that."

"Didn't work lassst time!" the python said, as its huge, long body slithered down the stairs toward him. "But give it your bessst shot."

Zeus braced himself, hoping that Ares was ready to attack from behind. Bolt sizzled in his hands.

Zap! A jagged streak of electricity hit the python. The snake flinched—and then its tail flicked out, knocking Bolt out of Zeus's hands.

"What elssse you got?" the snake hissed.

Then its head suddenly snapped around. "What was that?"

Ares had climbed the stairs on the other side of the temple and was standing at its entrance. The end of the python's tail waved in front of him. He swung back his spear. He had a clear shot.

Suddenly the snake's head zoomed in a flash to appear right in front of Ares.

"What do we have here?" the snake asked. It eyed the iron spear in Ares's hand. "A new toothpick for me?"

"This isn't a toothpick," Ares said, his red eyes flashing angrily. "It's the Spear of Fear. Now meet your doom!"

"I'll take that," the python said, quickly flicking out its long, red tongue.

Ares thought fast, unwilling to let the snake get his spear. He swiftly ducked, and then tore off running around the temple, the python's hot breath on his back as he ran.

"Don't be ssscared . . . ," hissed the python.

Hera and Apollo ran to meet Ares. Zeus trailed behind, carrying Bolt. The python's mouth opened wide. Zeus knew the snake could swallow Ares in one gulp. Was Zeus about to lose another Olympian?

The python's huge mouth started to close on Ares. But before it closed shut, the Spear of Fear came flying out. Apollo caught it.

"Apollo, use it!" Zeus yelled.

The python hiccuped and then licked his lips. "Delicioussss!"

Apollo acted quickly, hurling the spear at the python. The Spear of Fear didn't wobble or wiggle or hide. It sailed smoothly through the air and then hit the python's body.

Bam! The python's body popped like a big balloon. A huge whoosh of hot air escaped from

the snake. Ares flew from its jaws toward them, covered in green slime.

"He's alive!" Hera yelled.

Sssssssssssss. A loud hissing sound filled the air as the snake's body deflated. The powerful hissy wind picked up Zeus, Hera, Apollo, and Ares. They went flying through the air, yelling in surprise. As he tumbled in the wind, Zeus noticed Otus and Ephialtes below them, each one holding a handle of the giant urn!

Where did they come from? he wondered. But he had bigger things to worry about. The wind was carrying them right into that urn!

"Noooooo!" Zeus cried, but he couldn't fight the strong wind. The four Olympians landed inside the huge urn. Then darkness fell as the two Cronies closed the lid.

"This means war!" Ares yelled.

CHAPTER EIGHT

Trapped!

H a! Ha! Ha! Did you hear that?" Otus asked. "He thinks he's gonna fight us. But he's trapped!"

"Yeah," Ephialtes said. "Wait until our bosses see how smart we were, to come back here with the urn and wait for the Olympians. They were like sitting geese."

"You mean sitting ducks, I think," Otus corrected him. "Or is it turkeys, maybe?"

"Never mind," Ephialtes growled. "Let's get this urn back to the army." They began walking.

Inside the urn Hera banged her fist on the side. "Let us out, you crummy Cronies!"

Zeus sat up, dizzy from being shot through the air riding a hot snake hiss. The inside of the urn was warm, and so dark that he couldn't see a thing in front of him.

"Is everyone okay?" he called out.

"I'm fine," Apollo replied, and his voice seemed far away. "This urn seems to be very wide. I think it's bigger inside than outside."

"A magic urn," Zeus mused. That would explain why the two Cronies could carry it with four Olympians inside. Hmm. Olympians— Apollo and Hera had suspected that more of them might be in this urn.

"Is anybody else in here?" Zeus yelled.

"Bro!" Zeus heard the word right next to his

ear as someone knocked him back down with an excited tackle.

"Poseidon!" Zeus cried, jumping up and hugging him.

"Hey! Who stepped on my foot!" Hera complained.

"Me. I'm here too," said Hades. "Sorry, Hera."

"We're here too," answered the last two missing Olympians. Hera let out a happy squeal and made her way toward Demeter and Hestia's voices.

"So we're all back together," Zeus said, counting in his head. "Eight Olympians!"

"We've been stuck in here for days," moaned Hades. "And I know it's dark and everything, but I'd much rather be in the Underworld."

"I miss the fresh air." Demeter sighed. "The Crony army has been carrying us around. Otus and Ephialtes had the urn at first, but they kept dropping us."

"But they snitched the urn from the other Cronies yesterday after they got in trouble for losing the rest of you," said Hestia. "Now that they have all of us, they'll take us back to the army, and then right to King Cronus." Zeus felt her shiver with fear next to him as she said the name.

"How come you can't just climb to the top and get out?" Zeus asked. "Hestia, you've got your torch, and Demeter's got magic seeds, and Poseidon, your trident could easily blow the lid off this thing."

"It could, if magic worked in here," Poseidon replied. "But it doesn't."

"He's right," Hera said. "I can't get Chip to do anything."

"Hey, Hera, can I have my helmet back?" Hades asked. "I know it's no use in here, but I've really missed it."

"Sure," Hera replied, and there were shuffling

sounds as she moved to find Hades in the dark of the urn.

"It's like when we were in the Underworld," Zeus realized. "Our magical objects didn't work there, either."

He sat down on the bottom of the urn. Things seemed hopeless. Those clumsy Cronies were going to deliver them right to the king! That wasn't how it was supposed to work. The Olympians were supposed to fight King Cronus and defeat him.

Pythia had told Zeus that he was the leader of the Olympians. As their leader he should know what to do. But right now he was out of ideas.

The Olympians were quiet for a while, thinking about their fate. They kept bumping into one another as the clumsy Cronies carried the urn over the countryside.

Finally, after what must have been hours, the Olympians felt the urn being set down.

"My tummy's grumbling!" they could hear Otus complain.

"Mine too," agreed Ephialtes. "Start the fire so we can heat up the stew."

"They're not the only hungry ones," mumbled Ares.

"We've been surviving off the food in our packs but we've run out," explained Hestia. "The Cronies haven't given us anything."

Ares stomped his foot. "That is totally unfair! Even in war you're supposed to feed your prisoners. Let's revolt."

Zeus sat up. "Hey, that's not a bad idea! Let's get loud and demand some dinner. If they open the lid to feed us or just tell us no, we might have a chance to escape."

"Not a bad plan, Boltbrain," Hera admitted.

She started pounding on the side of the urn. "We want food! Prisoners' rights!"

"Yeah, King Cronus will be mad if we starve to death before you feed us to him!" Poseidon added.

"We want food! We want food! We want food!" Apollo began to chant, and the other Olympians joined him.

Outside the urn the Cronies just laughed.

"Don't worry, Olympians," Ephialtes said loudly. "We'll get you to King Cronus by morning. You won't starve."

Apollo stopped chanting, and the others followed his lead—except Ares. He wouldn't give up. He pounded on the side of the urn and yelled until his voice was hoarse.

Zeus finally put an arm on his shoulder. "It's not going to work, Ares," he said. "But don't worry. We'll think of something else."

"Well, you'd better think fast," Ares mumbled, but he'd stopped yelling.

Hera moved to be next to Zeus. "So, what's the plan now?"

"I don't know," Zeus admitted. "If we can't escape, we're going to need a battle plan once we get to King Cronus. We won't go down without a fight."

"I like the sound of that," agreed Ares.

Zeus yawned. It had to be nighttime by now, he guessed. They hadn't felt the urn move in a while.

Zzzzzzzz.

A loud snoring sound came from outside the urn.

"Do they snore like that every night?" Ares asked.

"No," replied Hades. "Most nights it's even louder."

"We don't need to sleep anyway," Zeus said. "Everybody gather around. We need a battle plan for the morning."

The Olympians huddled up. Zeus still could barely see, but it felt good to have everyone together again.

"Okay," he said. "First we need to tell Hestia, Demeter, and Hades about the new magical object. It belongs to Ares, and it's the Spear of Fear."

"Sounds cool!" said Hades. "How did you get it?"

"Well—" Ares began.

As Ares talked, Zeus felt himself dozing off. Suddenly he was jolted awake. "Wha—?" he asked, momentarily confused.

Hera shushed him. "Listen!" she hissed.

A female voice was talking in a loud whisper outside the urn.

"Olympians! Can you hear me?"

"We hear you!" Zeus called back.

"I am Rhea," the voice said, and Zeus felt a chill go through him.

Rhea?

Rhea was his mother—the mother he had never met. The mother he had been looking for his whole life! And she was the mother of most of the other Olympians too.

Stunned, the Olympians went silent.

"Know that I am proud of you all," Rhea continued. "I'm doing what I do now only to keep you safe. It is the only way to save you from being delivered to King Cronus. Trust me."

"Wait!" Zeus cried. "Don't go!"

Suddenly they all went flying as the urn got turned over onto its side. The Olympians all yelled as they crashed into one another. Zeus could feel the urn rolling, moving faster and faster.

"She pushed us down a hill!" he shouted.

CHAPTER NINE

Lost and Found

Aaaaaaaahhhhhh!"

The Olympians screamed as the urn bumped and thumped its way down the hill. Then it came to an abrupt halt as it crashed into something hard—a boulder!

The urn broke into pieces, sending the Olympians shooting in all directions. Zeus glanced down and saw a rushing river below him. Yikes! Just before he was about to hit the water, he quickly tossed Bolt toward the shore.

Splash! Splash! Splash! One by one the Olympians landed in the river. Zeus tried to get his bearings and swim, but the swift water pushed him down the river. He might as well have been a leaf bobbing along.

"Is everyone okay?" he asked, sputtering as he inhaled some river water. If anyone answered, he couldn't hear them over the rushing water. He wasn't even sure if they could hear him.

Finally the water started to slow, and Zeus could see the heads of the others bobbing on top of the water. The current washed all of them up onto the riverbank, out of the water and onto dry land.

"Bolt, return!" Zeus called out, and his magical weapon flew to him in an instant. Drenched and weary, he sat up. The other Olympians were slowly sitting up around him.

"How's everybody doing?" he asked. "Do we still have all our magical objects?"

Ares ran up to him, his eyes shining. He was still holding a spear, but it didn't look like the old Spear of Fear. Now it had a narrow, elm-shaped point made of gleaming bronze, with a sharp bronze spike on the other end. The handle of the spear was made of polished, flexible wood.

"It changed!" Ares cried. "How did that happen?"

"Well, maybe you and the spear bonded," Zeus guessed. "You used good strategy back there, fighting the python. It was smart throwing the spear to Apollo."

"Yeah, it was," Ares agreed proudly. He got into a fighting stance and started jabbing the spear in the air. "Take that! And that!"

"Be careful with that thing," Hera warned, ducking him as she searched the riverbank. "I think I lost my peacock feather in the river."

It was pretty, but at least you didn't lose a magical object or anything," said Demeter.

Apollo started to strum his lyre.

"The brave Olympians escaped the urn,
Thanks to a Titan named Rhea.
And now there is just one more thing to learn.
Where on earth is Pythia?"

As he strummed the last note, a crack opened up in the ground in front of him. Swirling mist poured from the crack, and a slender, dark-haired woman appeared inside the fog.

"Pythia!" Zeus cried.

Pythia adjusted her eyeglasses. "Yes, I am free again, thanks to you all," she said. "That snake was annoying. So full of hot air! Anyway, I see you escaped from the urn."

"Rhea freed us," Zeus informed her. "But for some reason she didn't stick around. Wouldn't she want to see her kids after all this time?"

"Your mother's heart is with you, although she cannot be with you herself," Pythia said.

"Why not?" Zeus asked, but Pythia had already turned to the others. "So, Hera, you finally found your magical object."

"You mean the aegis is mine?" Hera asked, surprised.

Pythia looked confused. "No, not the aegis. The Feather of Eyes is your magical object."

It was Hera's turn to look confused. Until she realized . . . "The peacock feather, you mean? That was my magical object?"

Pythia nodded, and Hera looked heartbroken.

"But I . . ." Her voice trailed off. She'd finally had her magical object, and then she'd lost it!

Before Hera could ask Pythia how to find it

again, Ares spoke up. "So what about the aegis, then? Is it mine?"

Pythia shook her head. "It partly belongs to Zeus. But he must share it with the new Olympian you've found."

"What new Olympian?" Zeus asked, puzzled.

Frowning, Pythia scanned the riverbank. "Oh, there she is. Step up, girl," she said, waving to someone. Then she turned back to the group. "Let me introduce you to Hyena, the goddess of foreverness!"

CHAPTER TEN

Sticky Spidernets!

A brown-haired girl with gray eyes stepped into the circle of confused Olympians.

"Actually, my name's Athena," she said. "Goddess of cleverness, not foreverness."

"Sorry about that," said Pythia. "Foggy spectacles can make seeing the future hard sometimes." She took them off to polish away the steamy mist. "You all can get to know one another later. Right now I must tell you of your next quest. I am not clear which magical object you will find this time, however."

"So, what do we do?" Zeus asked.

"First you must head to the center of a 'trouble spot,'" she reported. "You will know it when you find it. There you must cut the Threads of Dread down to size."

"Threads of Dread? What in the world are those?" Poseidon asked.

Zeus asked a question at the same time. "What about King Cronus? The Cronies said he was close by."

"And what about my feather?" Hera asked quickly. "What kind of magic can it do? And how can I find it again?"

But Pythia was already starting to fade away.

"You will have your answers soon enough . . . " she said, her voice trailing off.

With a final wave she disappeared.

"Noooo!" Hera wailed.

Hestia and Demeter walked up to Athena.

"Nice to meet you," Hestia said. "I'm—"

"Hestia," Athena said quickly. "I got to know all of you from your voices inside the urn. You're the protector of the hearth."

"You were in the urn with us all that time? Why didn't you let us know?" Demeter asked.

"Well, the urn was huge inside, so it was easy to hide," Athena said. "And I didn't know if I could trust any of you, so I figured it would be smart to just listen and gather information."

Hera put her hands on her hips. "So you were spying on us?"

"Not exactly," Athena said. Then she quickly

changed the subject. "Hey! Didn't you say some-thing about a lost feather?"

"Yeah!" Hera said. "And I am going back to search the length of that river for it. You guys don't have to come with me. I'll catch up to you." She started to march off.

Zeus ran after her and grabbed her arm. "You can't go alone! It's too dangerous. There are Cronies everywhere."

"I can take care of myself," Hera said fiercely.

"I know you can," Zeus said. "Probably better than any other Olympian. That's why we need you with us. We've got to stick to Pythia's plan. We've got to find the center of a trouble spot and cut the Threads of Dread. And we don't know where we're going, which is why we need you to show us the way with Chip."

Hera folded her arms smugly. "Oh, I don't need Chip to figure out where we need to head next," she said. She pointed to the sky behind Zeus and the others. Everyone turned around.

The morning sky was a pale shade of orange. Against it they could see the most massive spiderweb ever, strung high between the clouds.

"That's impossible," Hades said, his mouth hanging open.

As they stared at the web, tits woven strands started to move and change. At first, the Olympians weren't sure what was going on, but slowly words started appearing in the sky web:

Surrender, Olympians!

The Olympians gasped.

"Um, guys, are we sure we want to go *toward* that thing?" Poseidon asked nervously. "I mean, it looks— Aaaahhhhh!"

A strong, silky thread shot down from the sky and wrapped itself around Poseidon's ankle, yanking him away.

"Sticky spidernets!" he cried.

Zeus grabbed Bolt. "Bolt, large!" he commanded. As he ran to rescue Poseidon, another thread shot down and grabbed Hestia's ankle. Then another thread grabbed Demeter, and the next one grabbed Hera!

"Help!" they cried as the sticky threads dragged them away.

"What's happening?" Hades asked, catching up to Zeus as the two of them chased after the four captured Olympians. Apollo, Ares, and Athena followed at their heels.

"I don't know!" Zeus replied. "But I'm not going to lose any more Olympians—not again!"

Heart pounding, he raced off after his captured friends, on a new quest that was quickly turning out to be one sticky situation!